D0463333

MARVEL
GUARDIANS OF THE GALAXY®

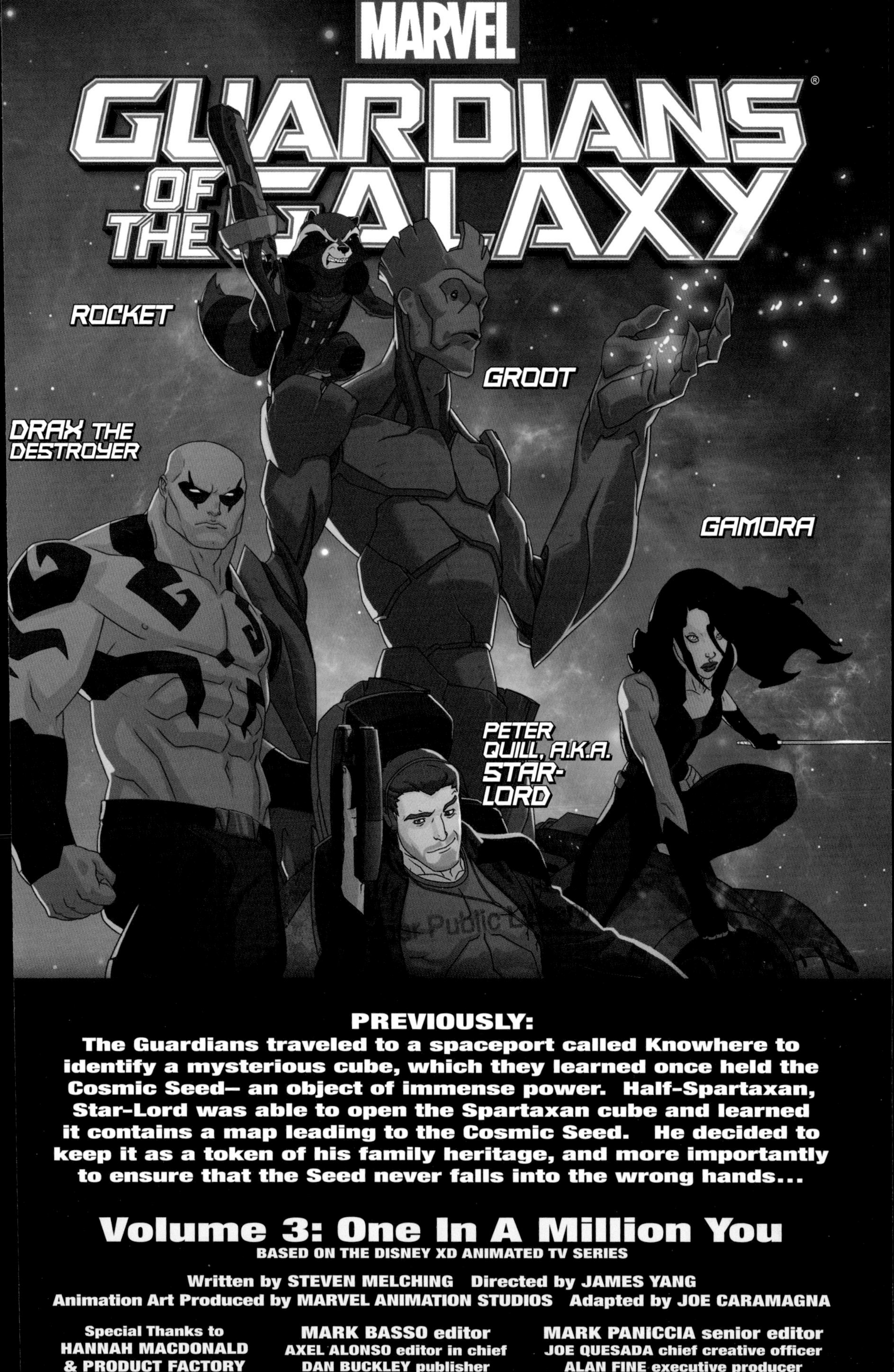
ROCKET
GROOT
DRAX THE DESTROYER
GAMORA
PETER QUILL, A.K.A. STAR-LORD

PREVIOUSLY:

The Guardians traveled to a spaceport called Knowhere to identify a mysterious cube, which they learned once held the Cosmic Seed– an object of immense power. Half-Spartaxan, Star-Lord was able to open the Spartaxan cube and learned it contains a map leading to the Cosmic Seed. He decided to keep it as a token of his family heritage, and more importantly to ensure that the Seed never falls into the wrong hands...

Volume 3: One In A Million You

BASED ON THE DISNEY XD ANIMATED TV SERIES

Written by STEVEN MELCHING Directed by JAMES YANG
Animation Art Produced by MARVEL ANIMATION STUDIOS Adapted by JOE CARAMAGNA

Special Thanks to HANNAH MACDONALD & PRODUCT FACTORY
MARK BASSO editor
AXEL ALONSO editor in chief
DAN BUCKLEY publisher
MARK PANICCIA senior editor
JOE QUESADA chief creative officer
ALAN FINE executive producer

ABDOPUBLISHING.COM

Reinforced library bound edition published in 2018 by Spotlight,
a division of ABDO, PO Box 398166, Minneapolis, Minnesota 55439.
Spotlight produces high-quality reinforced library bound editions for
schools and libraries. Published by agreement with Marvel Characters, Inc.

Printed in the United States of America, North Mankato, Minnesota.
042017
092017

THIS BOOK CONTAINS
RECYCLED MATERIALS

marvelkids.com
© 2017 MARVEL

PUBLISHER'S CATALOGING IN PUBLICATION DATA

Names: Melching, Steven ; Caramagna, Joe, authors. | Marvel Animation,
    illustrator.
Title: One in a million you / writers: Steven Melching ; Joe Caramagna ; art:
    Marvel Animation.
Description: Reinforced library bound edition. | Minneapolis, Minnesota : Spotlight,
    2018. | Series: Guardians of the galaxy ; volume 3
Summary: After the Guardians narrowly escape Thanos and Korath, Rocket accepts
    an offer to work for the Collector, while the other Guardians search for
    Pandorian crystals needed to power the map to the Cosmic Seed.
Identifiers: LCCN 2017931208 | ISBN 9781532140723 (lib. bdg.)
Subjects: LCSH: Superheroes--Juvenile fiction. | Adventure and adventurers--
    Juvenile fiction. | Comic books, strips, etc.--Juvenile fiction. | Graphic novels--
    Juvenile fiction.
Classification: DDC 741.5--dc23
LC record available at https://lccn.loc.gov/2017931208

Spotlight

A Division of ABDO
abdopublishing.com

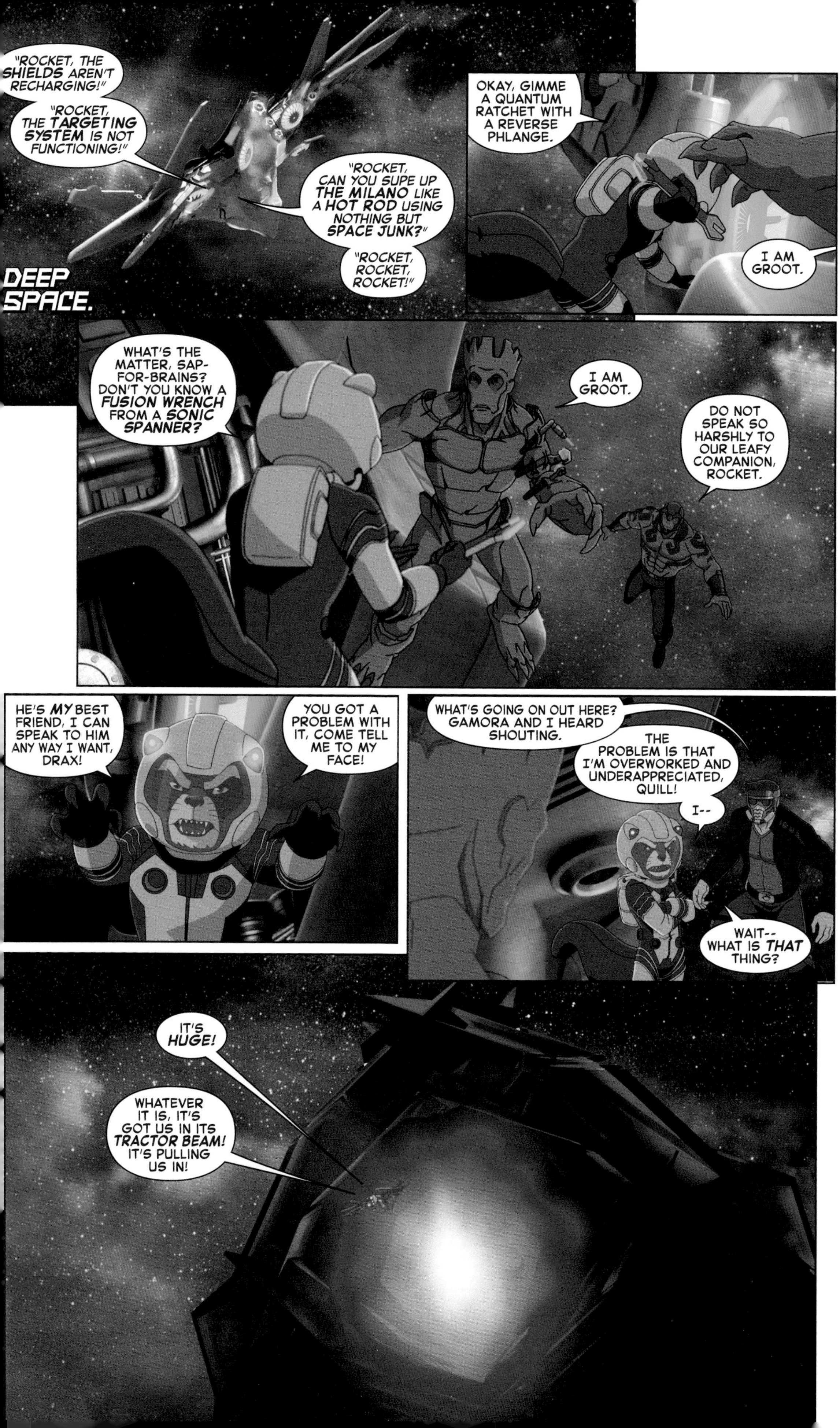
"ROCKET, THE SHIELDS AREN'T RECHARGING!"
"ROCKET, THE TARGETING SYSTEM IS NOT FUNCTIONING!"
"ROCKET, CAN YOU SUPE UP THE MILANO LIKE A HOT ROD USING NOTHING BUT SPACE JUNK?"
"ROCKET, ROCKET, ROCKET!"
DEEP SPACE.
OKAY, GIMME A QUANTUM RATCHET WITH A REVERSE PHLANGE.
I AM GROOT.
WHAT'S THE MATTER, SAP-FOR-BRAINS? DON'T YOU KNOW A FUSION WRENCH FROM A SONIC SPANNER?
I AM GROOT.
DO NOT SPEAK SO HARSHLY TO OUR LEAFY COMPANION, ROCKET.
HE'S MY BEST FRIEND, I CAN SPEAK TO HIM ANY WAY I WANT, DRAX!
YOU GOT A PROBLEM WITH IT, COME TELL ME TO MY FACE!
WHAT'S GOING ON OUT HERE? GAMORA AND I HEARD SHOUTING.
THE PROBLEM IS THAT I'M OVERWORKED AND UNDERAPPRECIATED, QUILL!
I--
WAIT-- WHAT IS THAT THING?
IT'S HUGE!
WHATEVER IT IS, IT'S GOT US IN ITS TRACTOR BEAM! IT'S PULLING US IN!

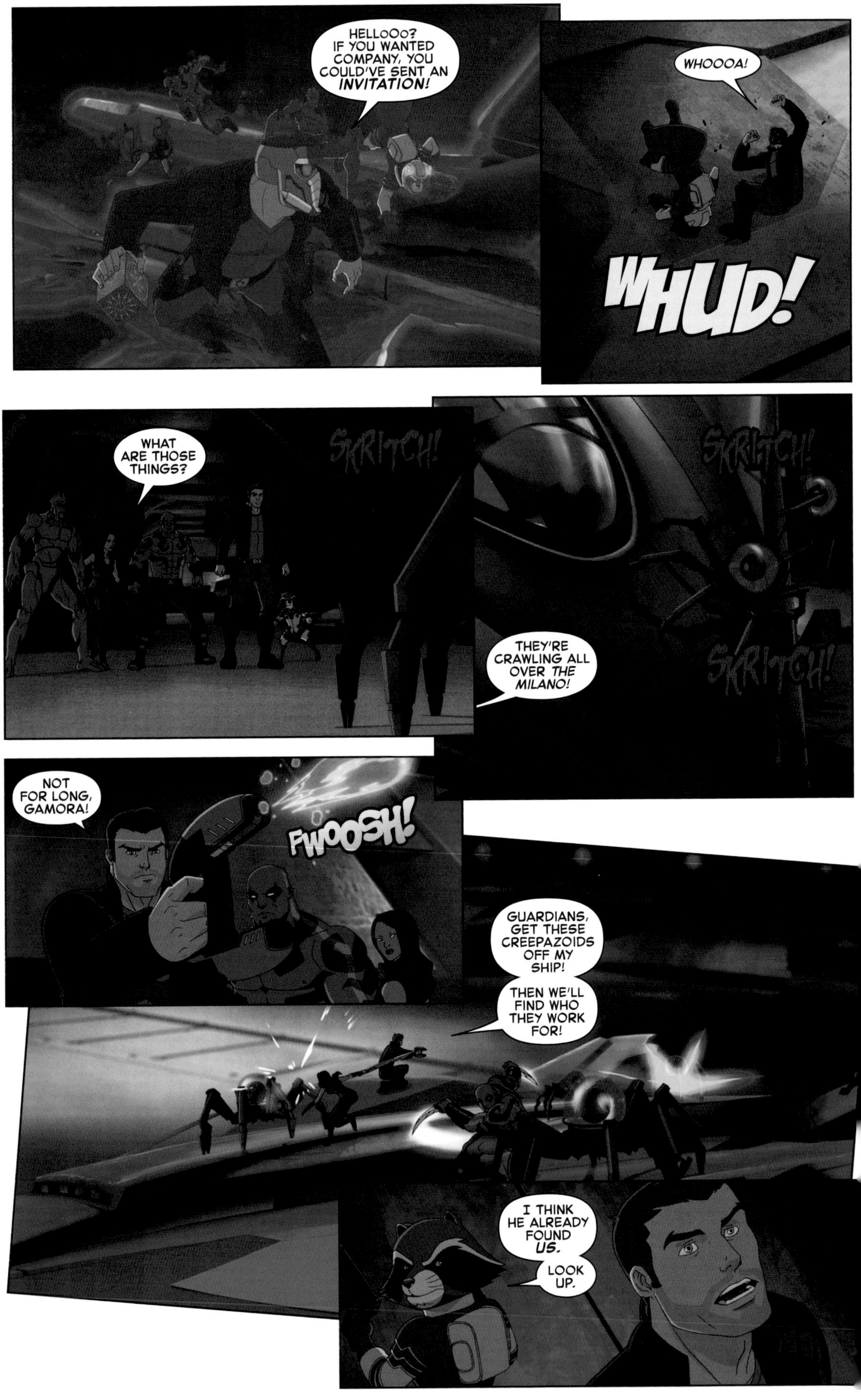
HELLOOO? IF YOU WANTED COMPANY, YOU COULD'VE SENT AN INVITATION!
WHOOOA!
WHUD!
WHAT ARE THOSE THINGS?
SKRITCH!
SKRITCH!
THEY'RE CRAWLING ALL OVER THE MILANO!
SKRITCH!
NOT FOR LONG, GAMORA!
FWOOSH!
GUARDIANS, GET THESE CREEPAZOIDS OFF MY SHIP!
THEN WE'LL FIND WHO THEY WORK FOR!
I THINK HE ALREADY FOUND US.
LOOK UP.

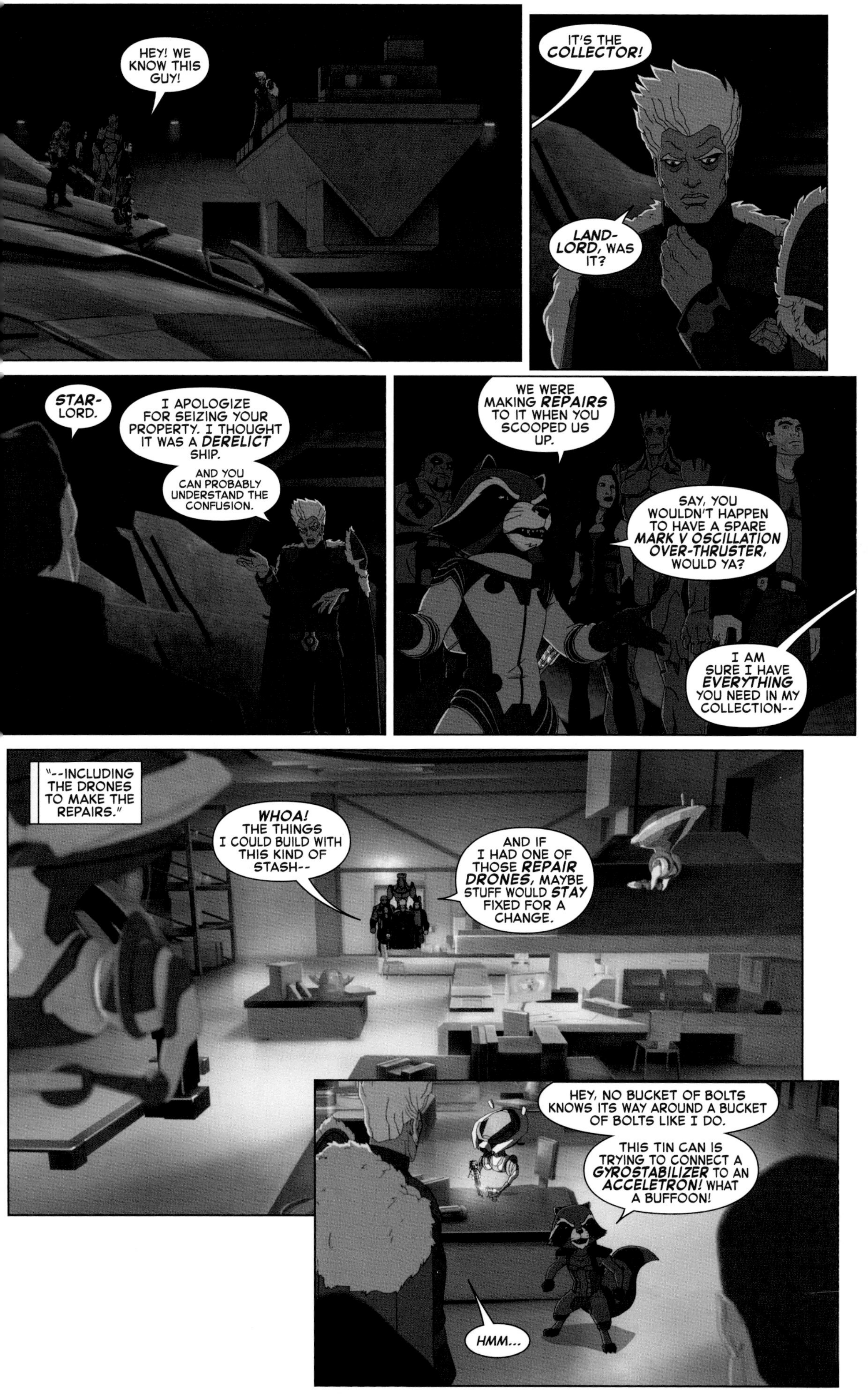
HEY! WE KNOW THIS GUY!
IT'S THE *COLLECTOR!*
LAND-LORD, WAS IT?
*STAR-*LORD.
I APOLOGIZE FOR SEIZING YOUR PROPERTY. I THOUGHT IT WAS A *DERELICT* SHIP.
AND YOU CAN PROBABLY UNDERSTAND THE CONFUSION.
WE WERE MAKING *REPAIRS* TO IT WHEN YOU SCOOPED US UP.
SAY, YOU WOULDN'T HAPPEN TO HAVE A SPARE *MARK V OSCILLATION OVER-THRUSTER,* WOULD YA?
I AM SURE I HAVE *EVERYTHING* YOU NEED IN MY COLLECTION--
"--INCLUDING THE DRONES TO MAKE THE REPAIRS."
WHOA! THE THINGS I COULD BUILD WITH THIS KIND OF STASH--
AND IF I HAD ONE OF THOSE *REPAIR DRONES,* MAYBE STUFF WOULD *STAY* FIXED FOR A CHANGE.
HEY, NO BUCKET OF BOLTS KNOWS ITS WAY AROUND A BUCKET OF BOLTS LIKE I DO.
THIS TIN CAN IS TRYING TO CONNECT A *GYROSTABILIZER* TO AN *ACCELETRON!* WHAT A BUFFOON!
HMM...

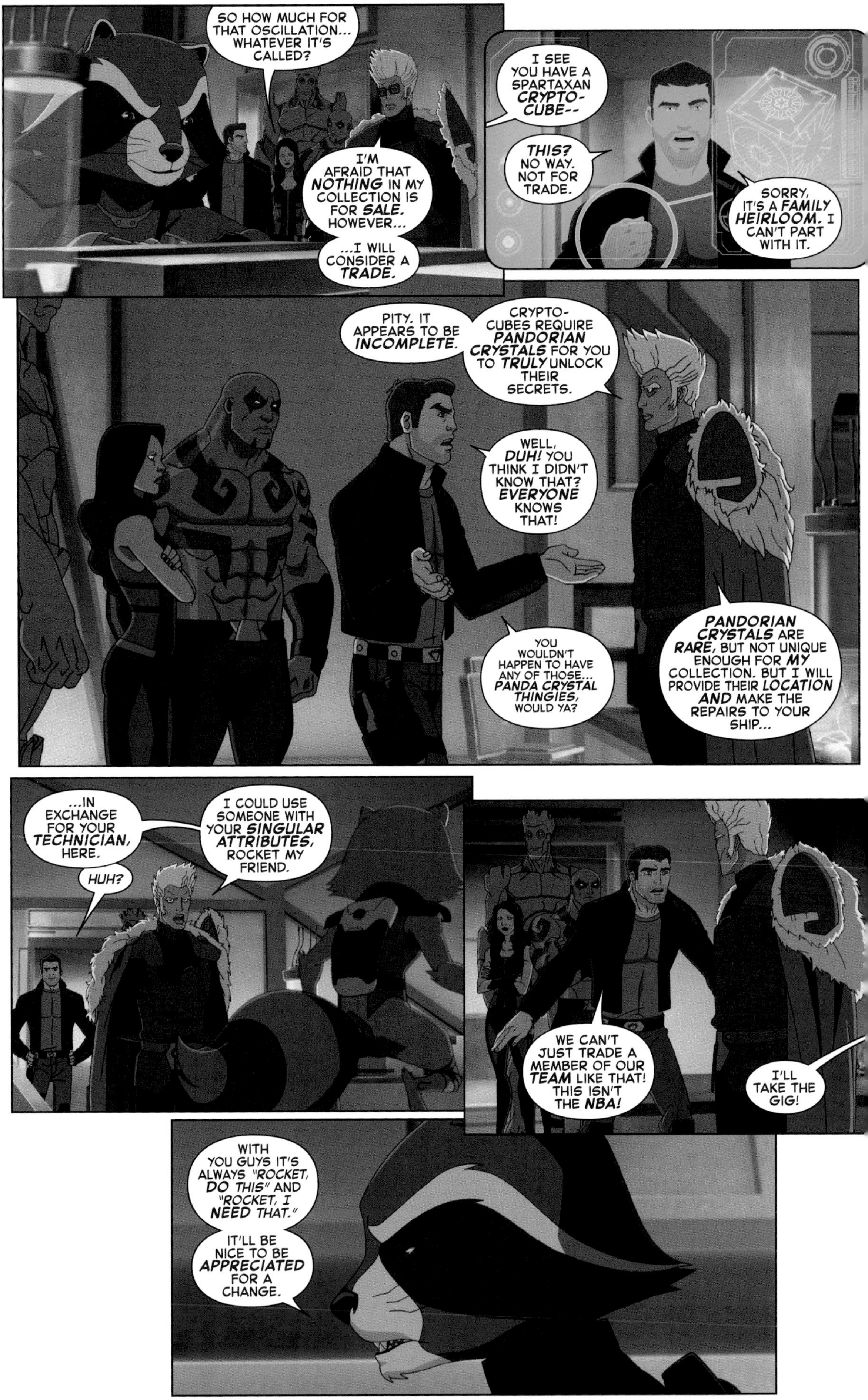

SO HOW MUCH FOR THAT OSCILLATION... WHATEVER IT'S CALLED?
I'M AFRAID THAT NOTHING IN MY COLLECTION IS FOR SALE. HOWEVER...
...I WILL CONSIDER A TRADE.
I SEE YOU HAVE A SPARTAXAN CRYPTO-CUBE--
THIS? NO WAY. NOT FOR TRADE.
SORRY, IT'S A FAMILY HEIRLOOM. I CAN'T PART WITH IT.
PITY. IT APPEARS TO BE INCOMPLETE.
CRYPTO-CUBES REQUIRE PANDORIAN CRYSTALS FOR YOU TO TRULY UNLOCK THEIR SECRETS.
WELL, DUH! YOU THINK I DIDN'T KNOW THAT? EVERYONE KNOWS THAT!
YOU WOULDN'T HAPPEN TO HAVE ANY OF THOSE... PANDA CRYSTAL THINGIES, WOULD YA?
PANDORIAN CRYSTALS ARE RARE, BUT NOT UNIQUE ENOUGH FOR MY COLLECTION. BUT I WILL PROVIDE THEIR LOCATION AND MAKE THE REPAIRS TO YOUR SHIP...
...IN EXCHANGE FOR YOUR TECHNICIAN, HERE.
I COULD USE SOMEONE WITH YOUR SINGULAR ATTRIBUTES, ROCKET MY FRIEND.
HUH?
WE CAN'T JUST TRADE A MEMBER OF OUR TEAM LIKE THAT! THIS ISN'T THE NBA!
I'LL TAKE THE GIG!
WITH YOU GUYS IT'S ALWAYS "ROCKET, DO THIS" AND "ROCKET, I NEED THAT."
IT'LL BE NICE TO BE APPRECIATED FOR A CHANGE.

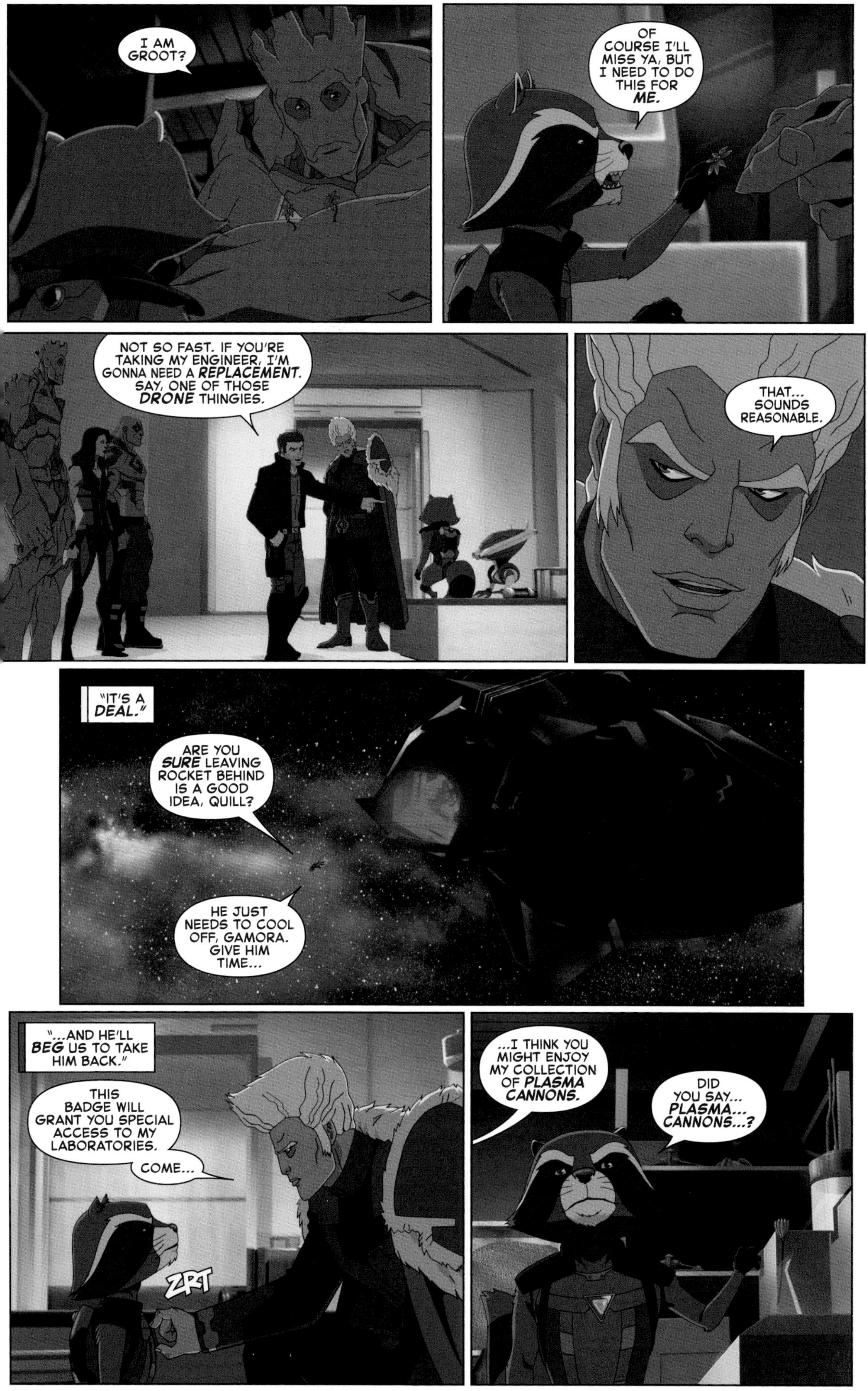
I AM GROOT?
OF COURSE I'LL MISS YA, BUT I NEED TO DO THIS FOR ME.
NOT SO FAST. IF YOU'RE TAKING MY ENGINEER, I'M GONNA NEED A REPLACEMENT. SAY, ONE OF THOSE DRONE THINGIES.
THAT... SOUNDS REASONABLE.
"IT'S A DEAL."
ARE YOU SURE LEAVING ROCKET BEHIND IS A GOOD IDEA, QUILL?
HE JUST NEEDS TO COOL OFF, GAMORA. GIVE HIM TIME...
"...AND HE'LL BEG US TO TAKE HIM BACK."
THIS BADGE WILL GRANT YOU SPECIAL ACCESS TO MY LABORATORIES.
COME...
ZRT
...I THINK YOU MIGHT ENJOY MY COLLECTION OF PLASMA CANNONS.
DID YOU SAY... PLASMA... CANNONS...?

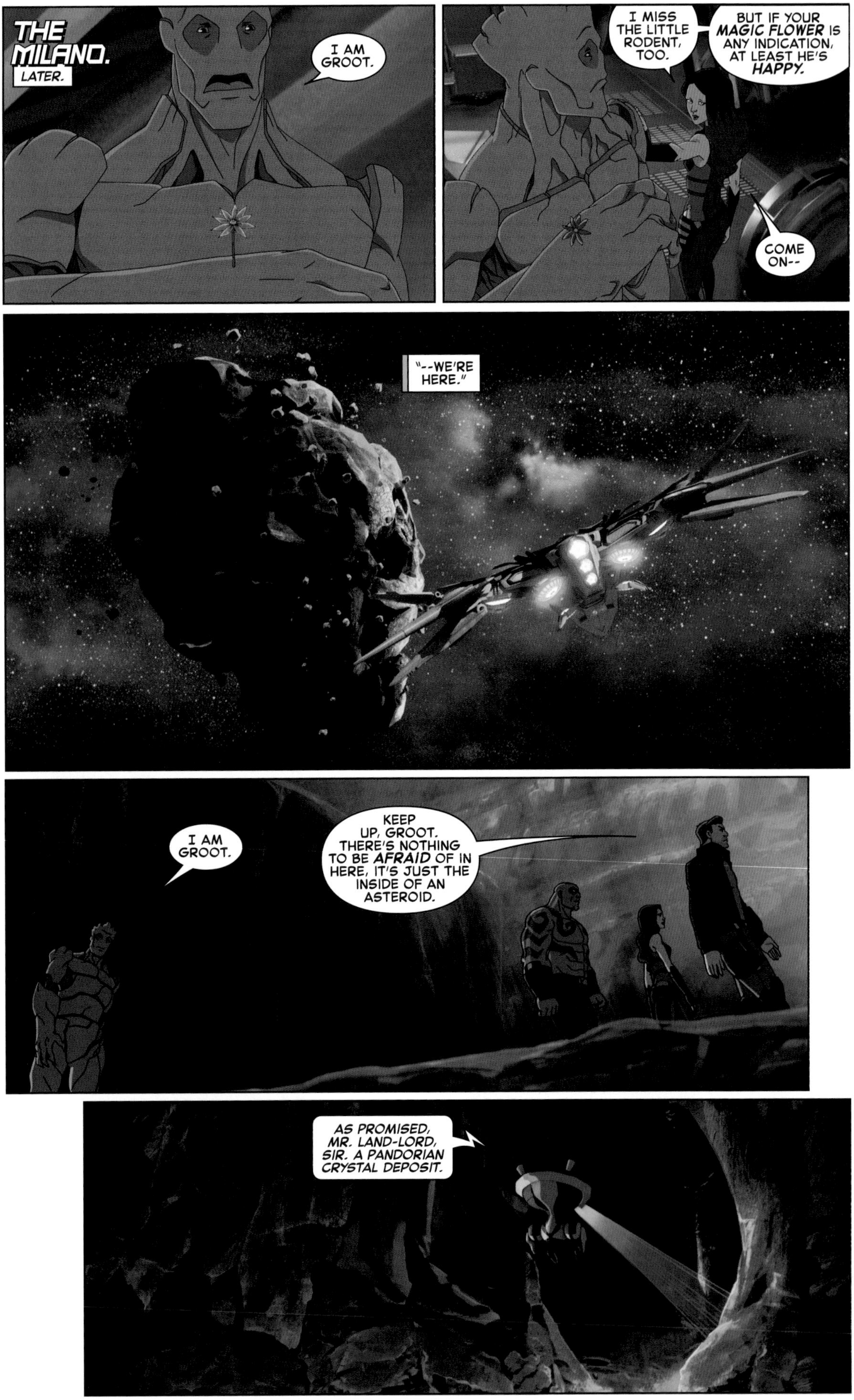
THE MILANO.
LATER.
I AM GROOT.
I MISS THE LITTLE RODENT, TOO.
BUT IF YOUR MAGIC FLOWER IS ANY INDICATION, AT LEAST HE'S HAPPY.
COME ON--
"--WE'RE HERE."
I AM GROOT.
KEEP UP, GROOT. THERE'S NOTHING TO BE AFRAID OF IN HERE, IT'S JUST THE INSIDE OF AN ASTEROID.
AS PROMISED, MR. LAND-LORD, SIR. A PANDORIAN CRYSTAL DEPOSIT.

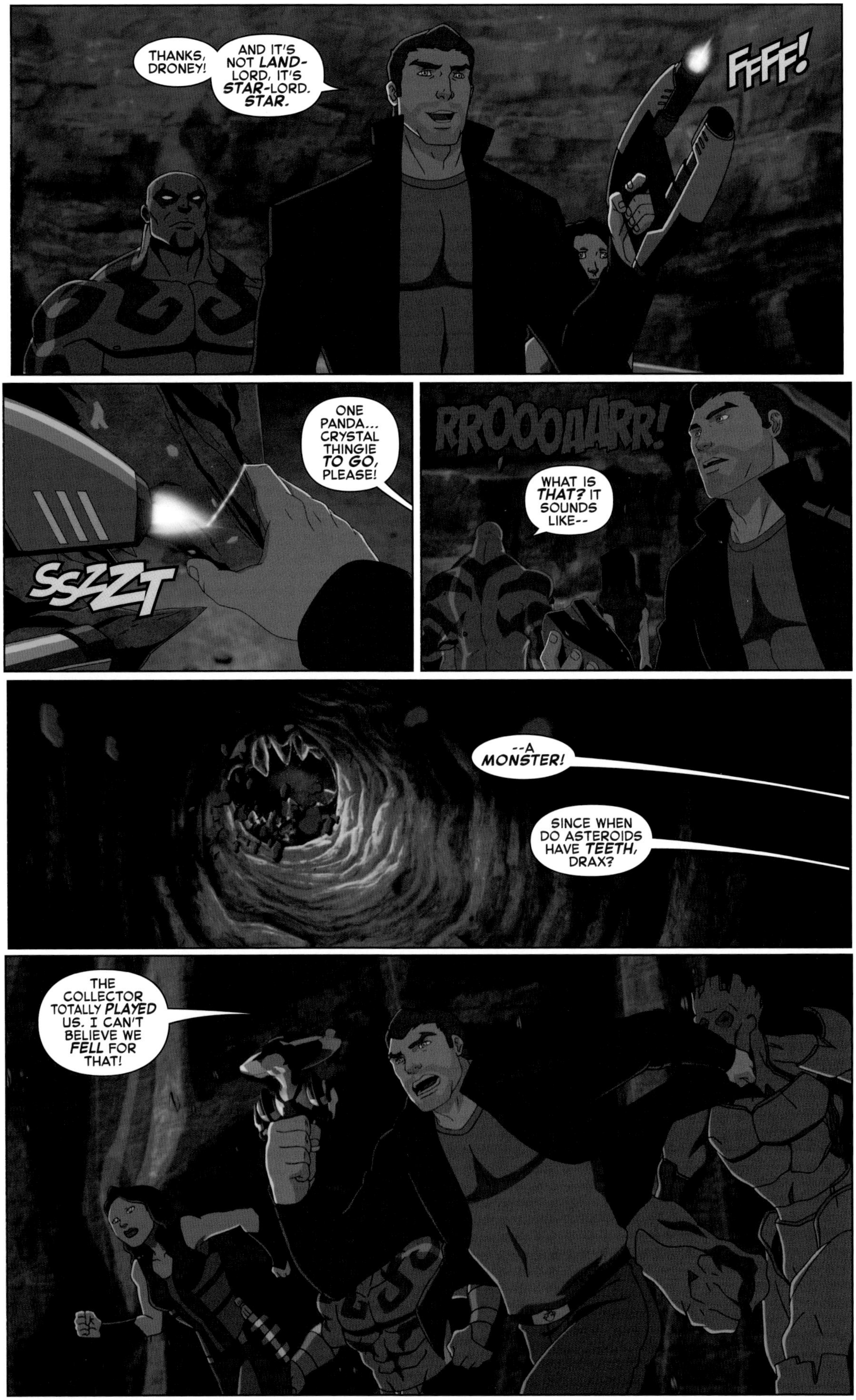
THANKS, DRONEY!
AND IT'S NOT LAND-LORD, IT'S STAR-LORD. STAR.
FFFF!
ONE PANDA... CRYSTAL THINGIE TO GO, PLEASE!
SSZZT
RROOOAARR!
WHAT IS THAT? IT SOUNDS LIKE--
--A MONSTER!
SINCE WHEN DO ASTEROIDS HAVE TEETH, DRAX?
THE COLLECTOR TOTALLY PLAYED US. I CAN'T BELIEVE WE FELL FOR THAT!

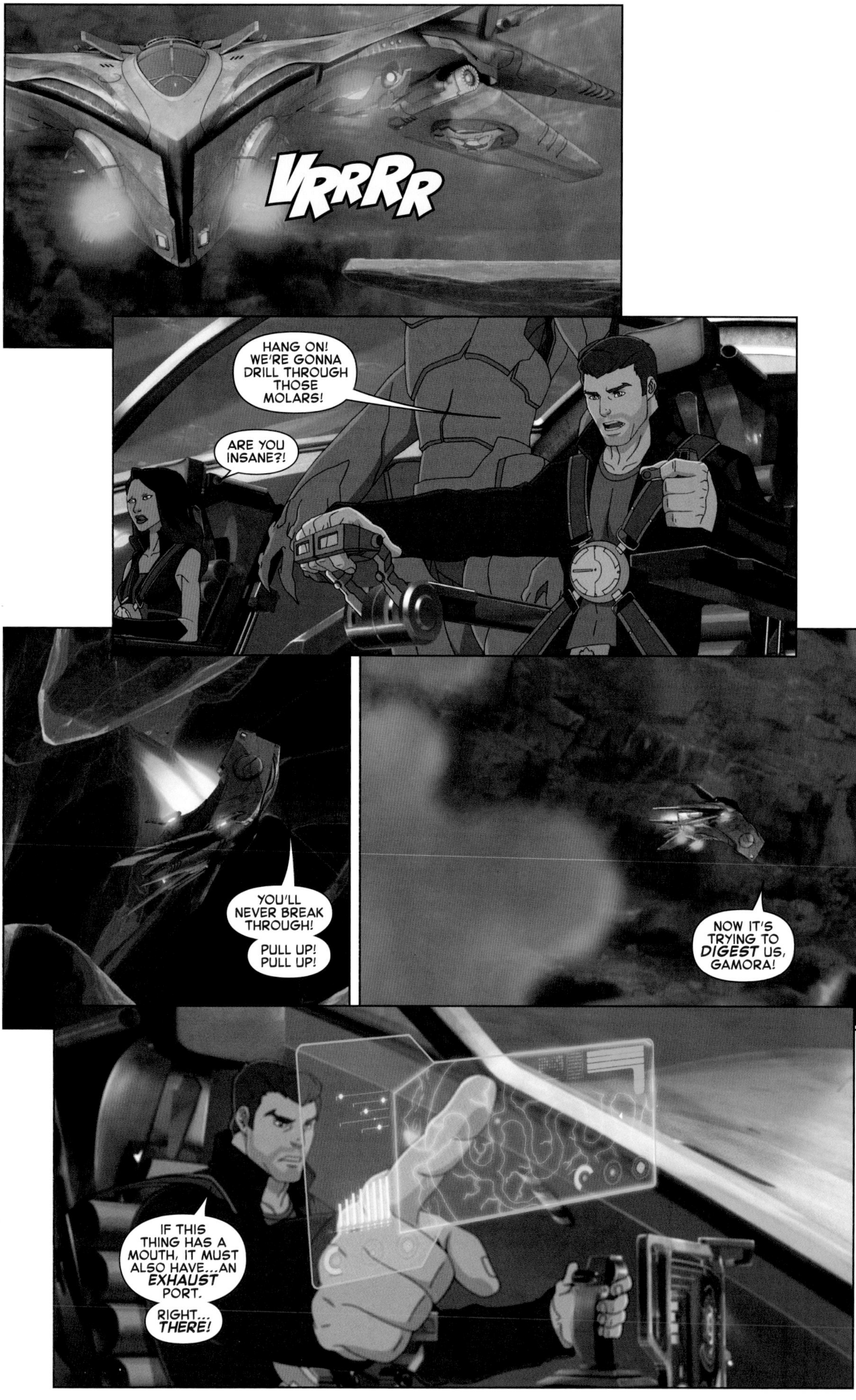
VRRRR
HANG ON! WE'RE GONNA DRILL THROUGH THOSE MOLARS!
ARE YOU INSANE?!
YOU'LL NEVER BREAK THROUGH!
PULL UP! PULL UP!
NOW IT'S TRYING TO DIGEST US, GAMORA!
IF THIS THING HAS A MOUTH, IT MUST ALSO HAVE...AN EXHAUST PORT.
RIGHT... THERE!

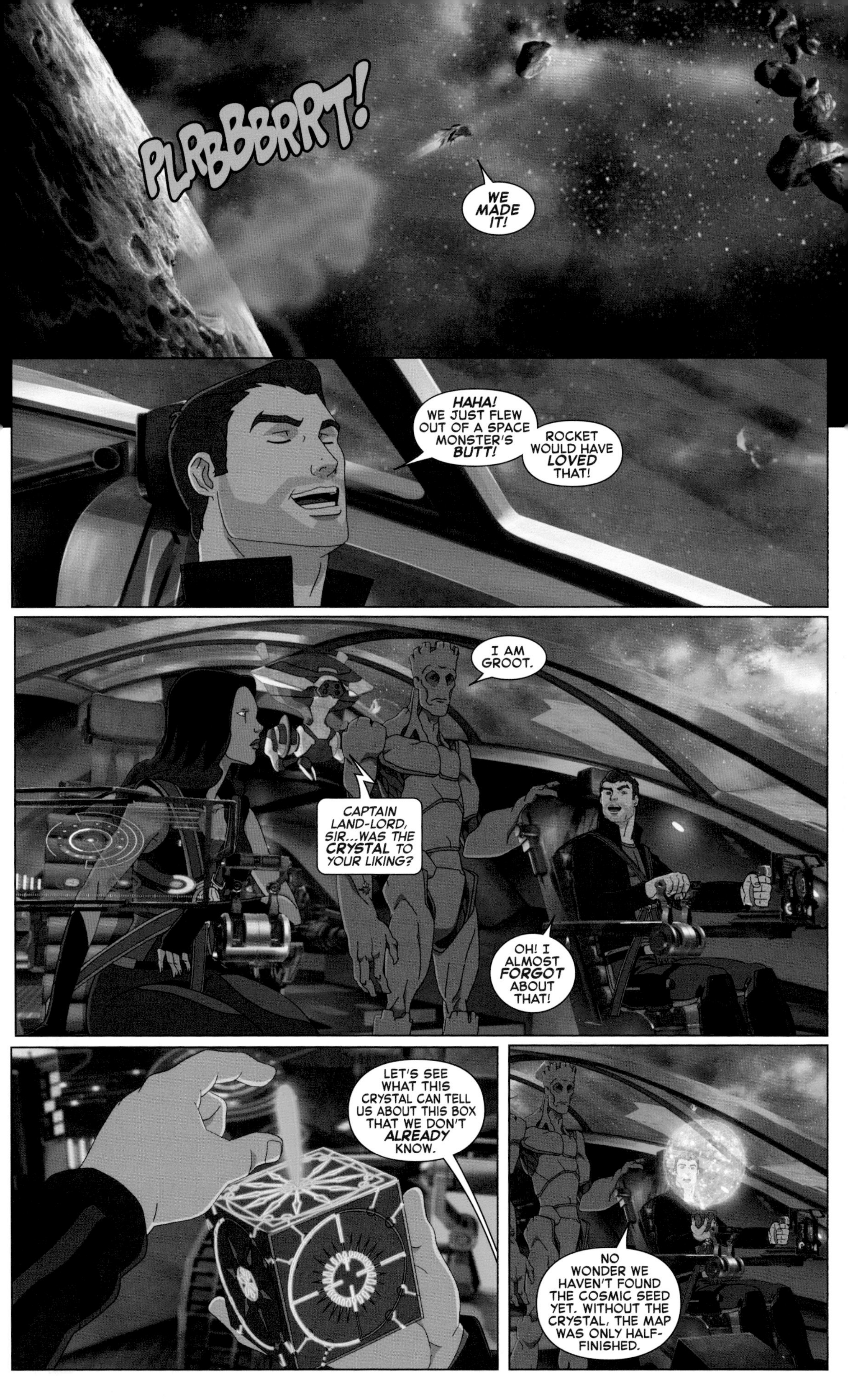
PLRBBBRRT!
WE MADE IT!
HAHA! WE JUST FLEW OUT OF A SPACE MONSTER'S BUTT!
ROCKET WOULD HAVE LOVED THAT!
I AM GROOT.
CAPTAIN LAND-LORD, SIR...WAS THE CRYSTAL TO YOUR LIKING?
OH! I ALMOST FORGOT ABOUT THAT!
LET'S SEE WHAT THIS CRYSTAL CAN TELL US ABOUT THIS BOX THAT WE DON'T ALREADY KNOW.
NO WONDER WE HAVEN'T FOUND THE COSMIC SEED YET. WITHOUT THE CRYSTAL, THE MAP WAS ONLY HALF-FINISHED.

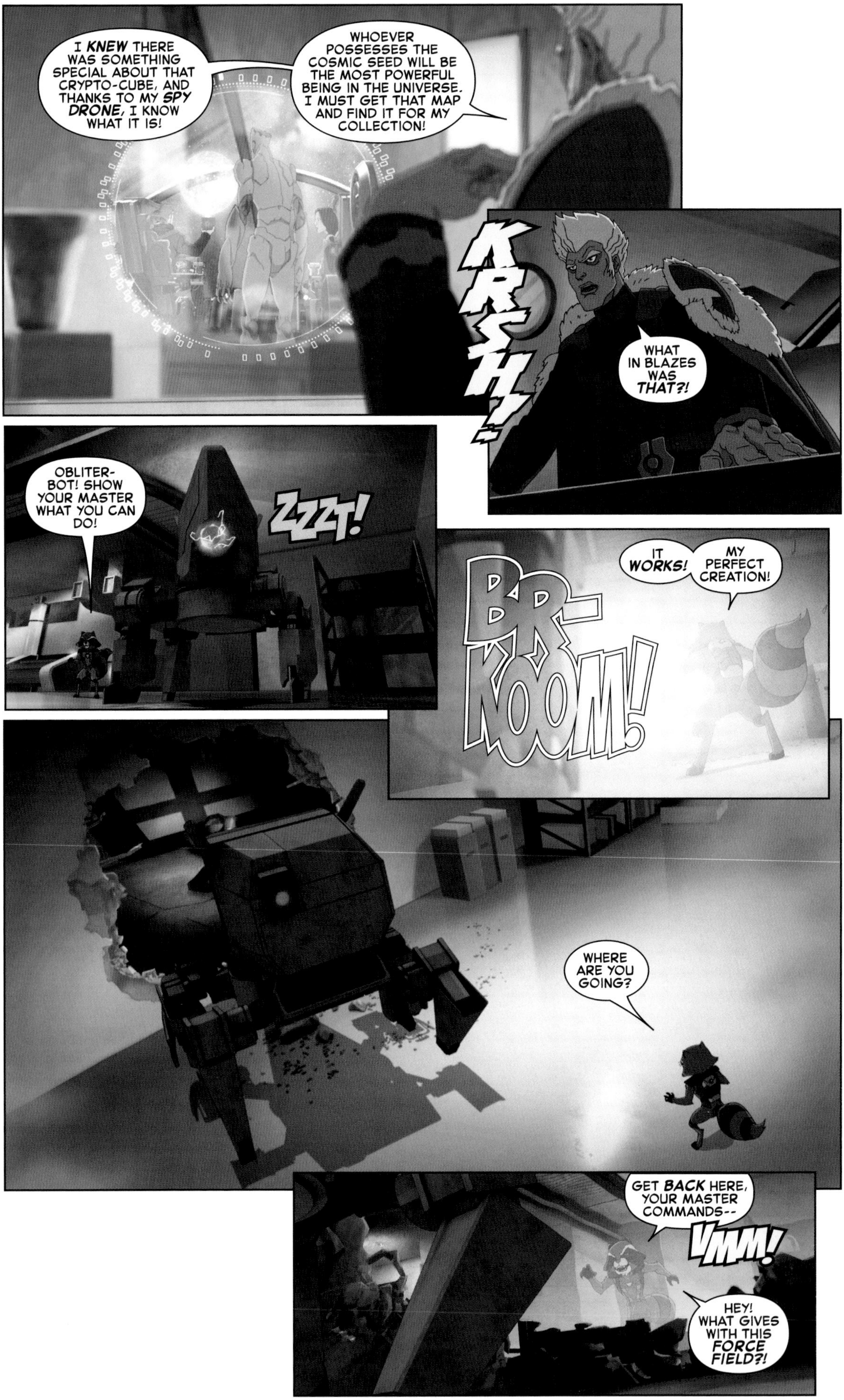
I KNEW THERE WAS SOMETHING SPECIAL ABOUT THAT CRYPTO-CUBE, AND THANKS TO MY SPY DRONE, I KNOW WHAT IT IS!
WHOEVER POSSESSES THE COSMIC SEED WILL BE THE MOST POWERFUL BEING IN THE UNIVERSE. I MUST GET THAT MAP AND FIND IT FOR MY COLLECTION!
KRSH!
WHAT IN BLAZES WAS THAT?!
OBLITER-BOT! SHOW YOUR MASTER WHAT YOU CAN DO!
ZZZT!
IT WORKS!
MY PERFECT CREATION!
BR-KOOM!
WHERE ARE YOU GOING?
GET BACK HERE, YOUR MASTER COMMANDS--
VMM!
HEY! WHAT GIVES WITH THIS FORCE FIELD?!

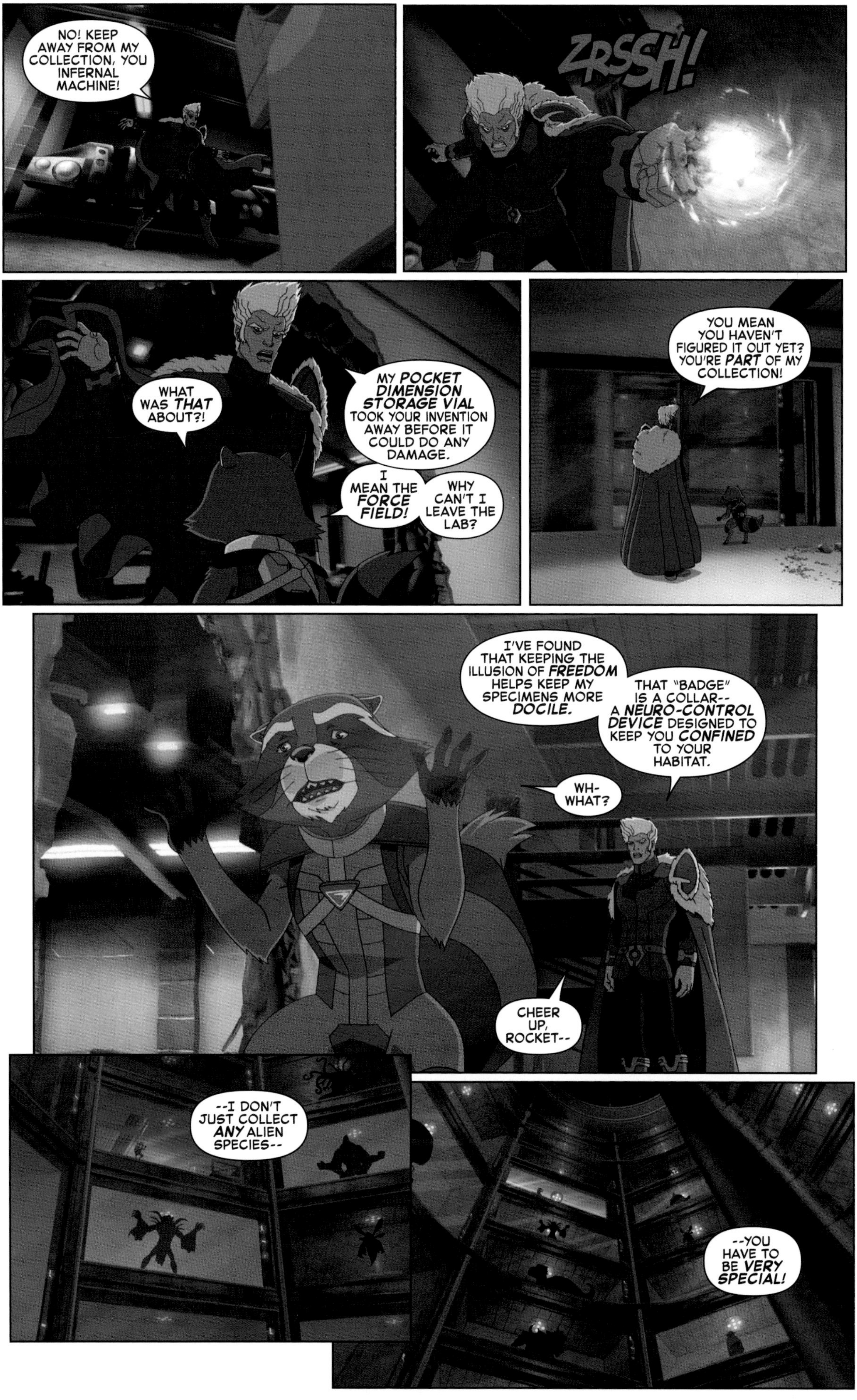
NO! KEEP AWAY FROM MY COLLECTION, YOU INFERNAL MACHINE!
ZRSSH!
WHAT WAS THAT ABOUT?!
MY POCKET DIMENSION STORAGE VIAL TOOK YOUR INVENTION AWAY BEFORE IT COULD DO ANY DAMAGE.
I MEAN THE FORCE FIELD!
WHY CAN'T I LEAVE THE LAB?
YOU MEAN YOU HAVEN'T FIGURED IT OUT YET? YOU'RE PART OF MY COLLECTION!
I'VE FOUND THAT KEEPING THE ILLUSION OF FREEDOM HELPS KEEP MY SPECIMENS MORE DOCILE.
THAT "BADGE" IS A COLLAR-- A NEURO-CONTROL DEVICE DESIGNED TO KEEP YOU CONFINED TO YOUR HABITAT.
WH-WHAT?
CHEER UP, ROCKET--
--I DON'T JUST COLLECT ANY ALIEN SPECIES--
--YOU HAVE TO BE VERY SPECIAL!

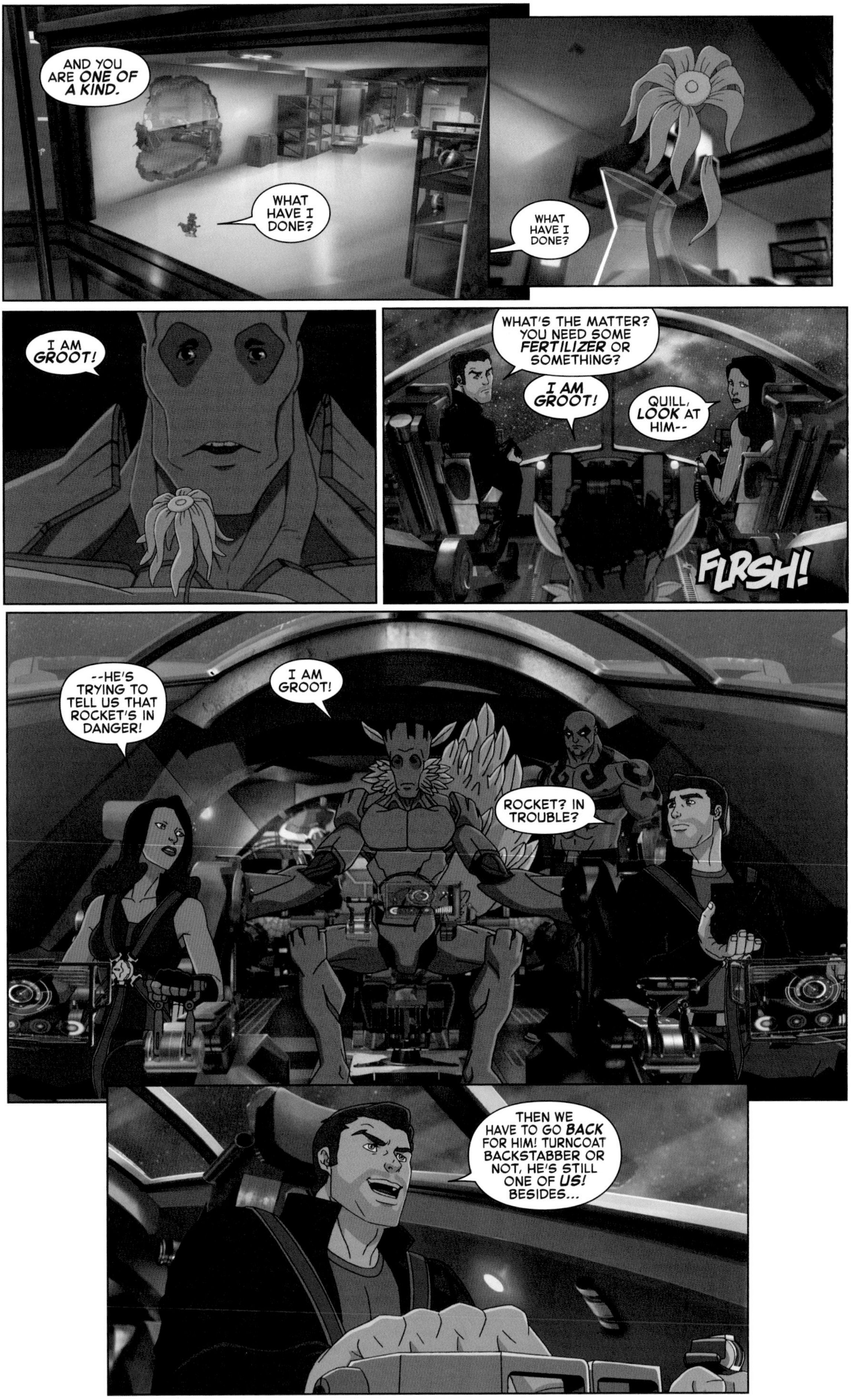
AND YOU ARE ONE OF A KIND.
WHAT HAVE I DONE?
WHAT HAVE I DONE?
I AM GROOT!
WHAT'S THE MATTER? YOU NEED SOME FERTILIZER OR SOMETHING?
I AM GROOT!
QUILL, LOOK AT HIM--
FLRSH!
--HE'S TRYING TO TELL US THAT ROCKET'S IN DANGER!
I AM GROOT!
ROCKET? IN TROUBLE?
THEN WE HAVE TO GO BACK FOR HIM! TURNCOAT BACKSTABBER OR NOT, HE'S STILL ONE OF US! BESIDES...

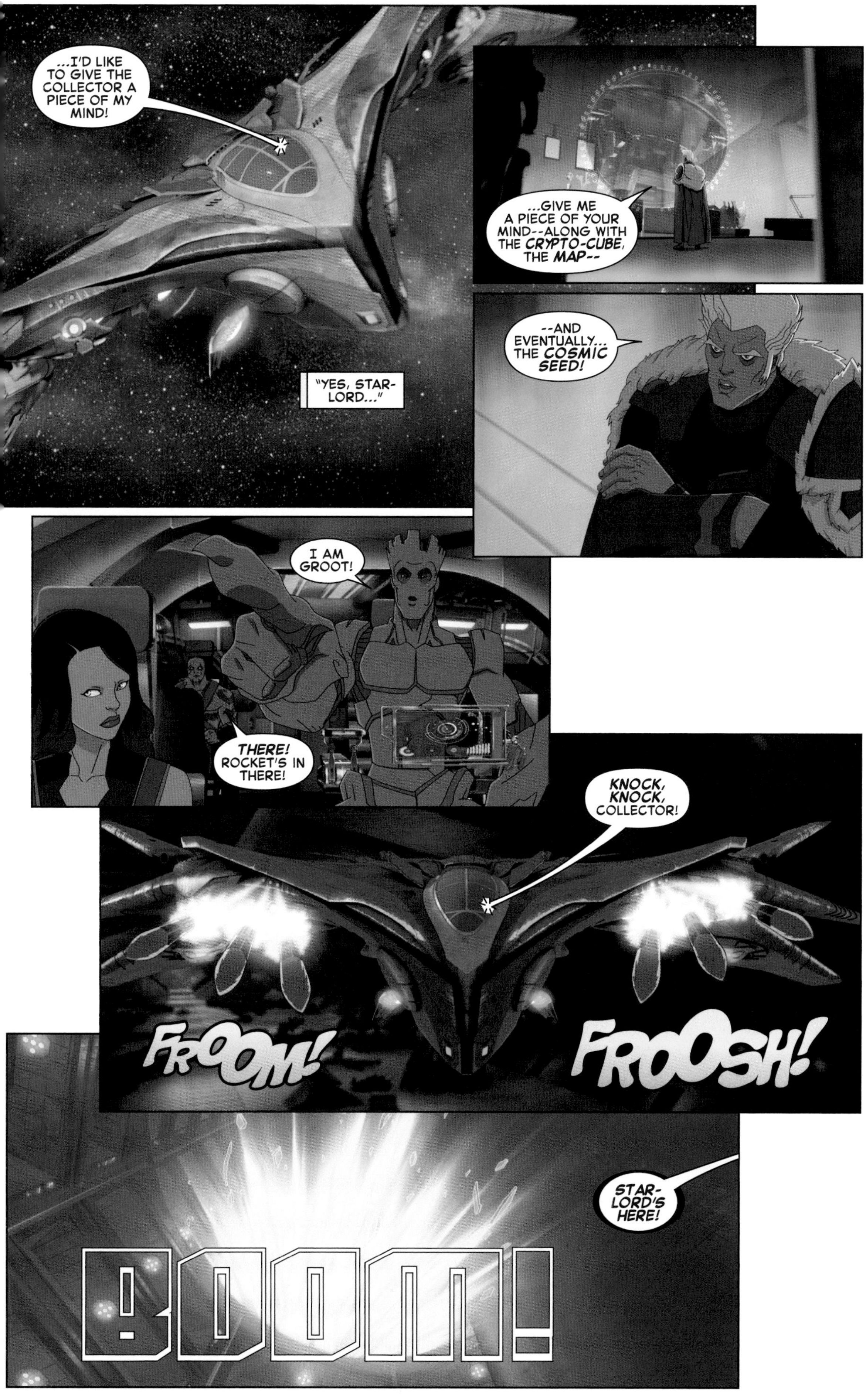
...I'D LIKE TO GIVE THE COLLECTOR A PIECE OF MY MIND!
"YES, STAR-LORD..."
...GIVE ME A PIECE OF YOUR MIND--ALONG WITH THE CRYPTO-CUBE, THE MAP--
--AND EVENTUALLY... THE COSMIC SEED!
I AM GROOT!
THERE! ROCKET'S IN THERE!
KNOCK, KNOCK, COLLECTOR!
FROOM!
FROOSH!
STAR-LORD'S HERE!
BOOM!

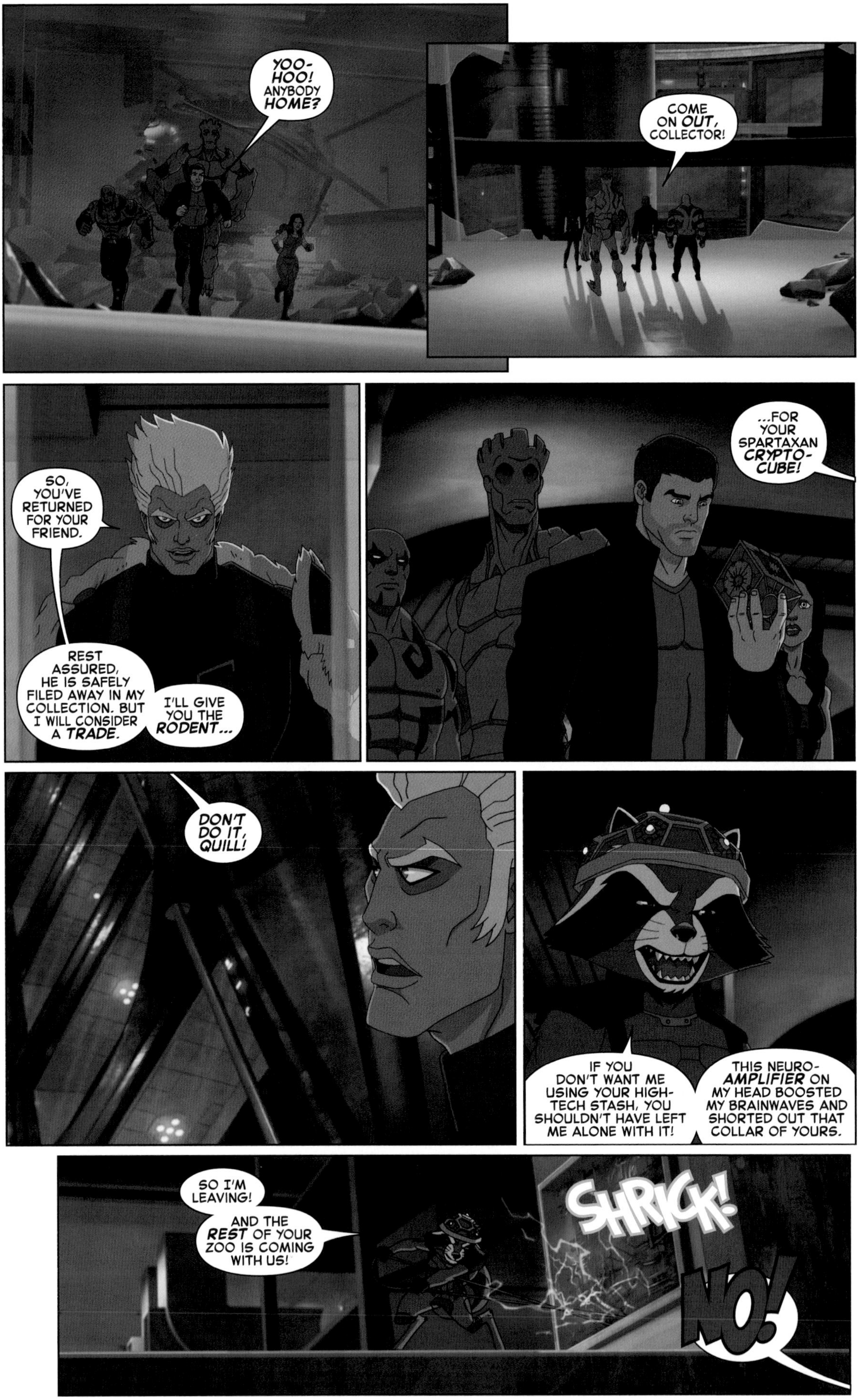
YOO-HOO! ANYBODY HOME?
COME ON OUT, COLLECTOR!
SO, YOU'VE RETURNED FOR YOUR FRIEND.
REST ASSURED, HE IS SAFELY FILED AWAY IN MY COLLECTION. BUT I WILL CONSIDER A TRADE.
I'LL GIVE YOU THE RODENT...
...FOR YOUR SPARTAXAN CRYPTO-CUBE!
DON'T DO IT, QUILL!
IF YOU DON'T WANT ME USING YOUR HIGH-TECH STASH, YOU SHOULDN'T HAVE LEFT ME ALONE WITH IT!
THIS NEURO-AMPLIFIER ON MY HEAD BOOSTED MY BRAINWAVES AND SHORTED OUT THAT COLLAR OF YOURS.
SO I'M LEAVING!
AND THE REST OF YOUR ZOO IS COMING WITH US!
SHRICK!
NO!

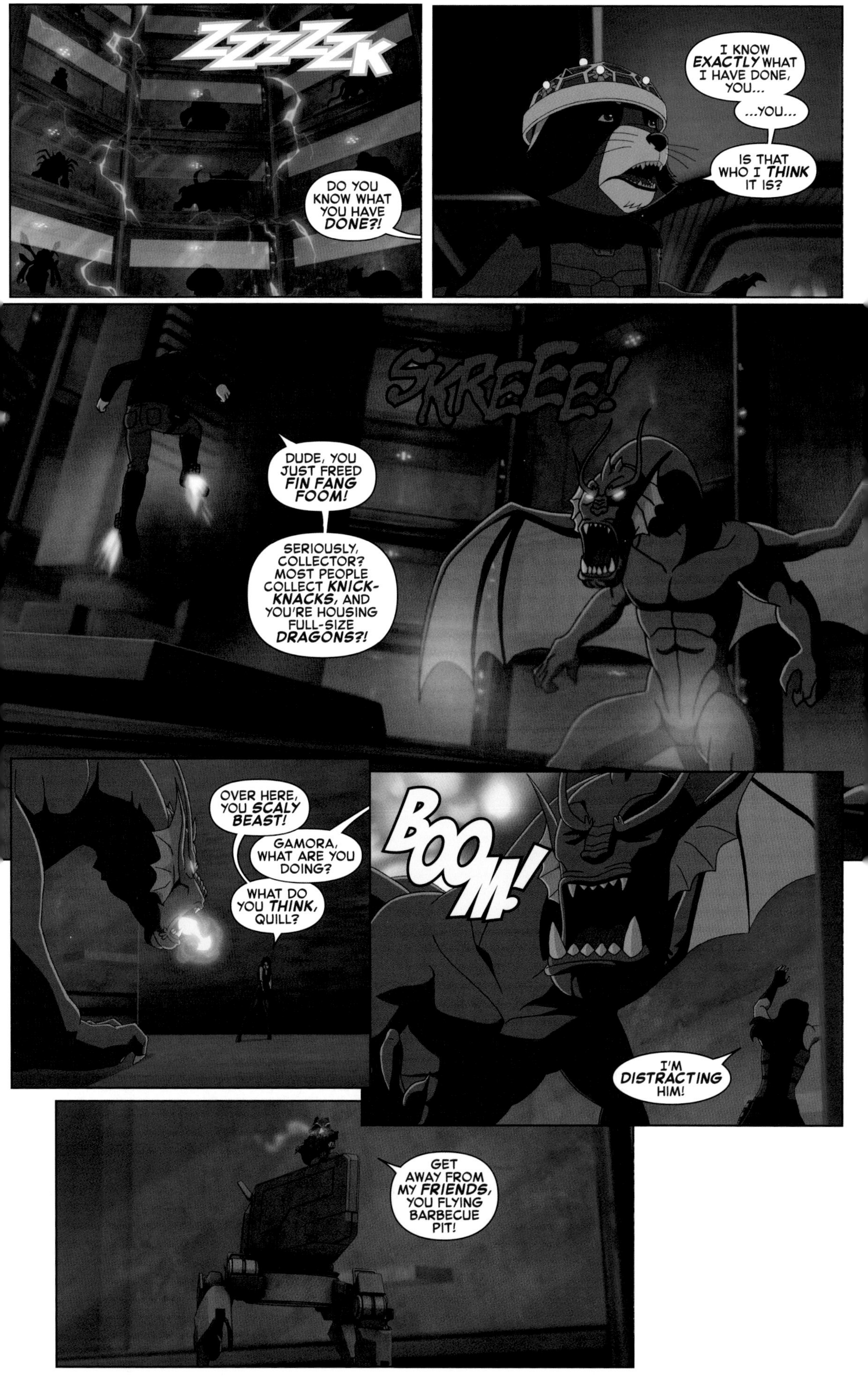
ZZZZZZK
DO YOU KNOW WHAT YOU HAVE DONE?!
I KNOW EXACTLY WHAT I HAVE DONE, YOU...
...YOU...
IS THAT WHO I THINK IT IS?
SKREEE!
DUDE, YOU JUST FREED FIN FANG FOOM!
SERIOUSLY, COLLECTOR? MOST PEOPLE COLLECT KNICK-KNACKS, AND YOU'RE HOUSING FULL-SIZE DRAGONS?!
OVER HERE, YOU SCALY BEAST!
GAMORA, WHAT ARE YOU DOING?
WHAT DO YOU THINK, QUILL?
BOOM!
I'M DISTRACTING HIM!
GET AWAY FROM MY FRIENDS, YOU FLYING BARBECUE PIT!

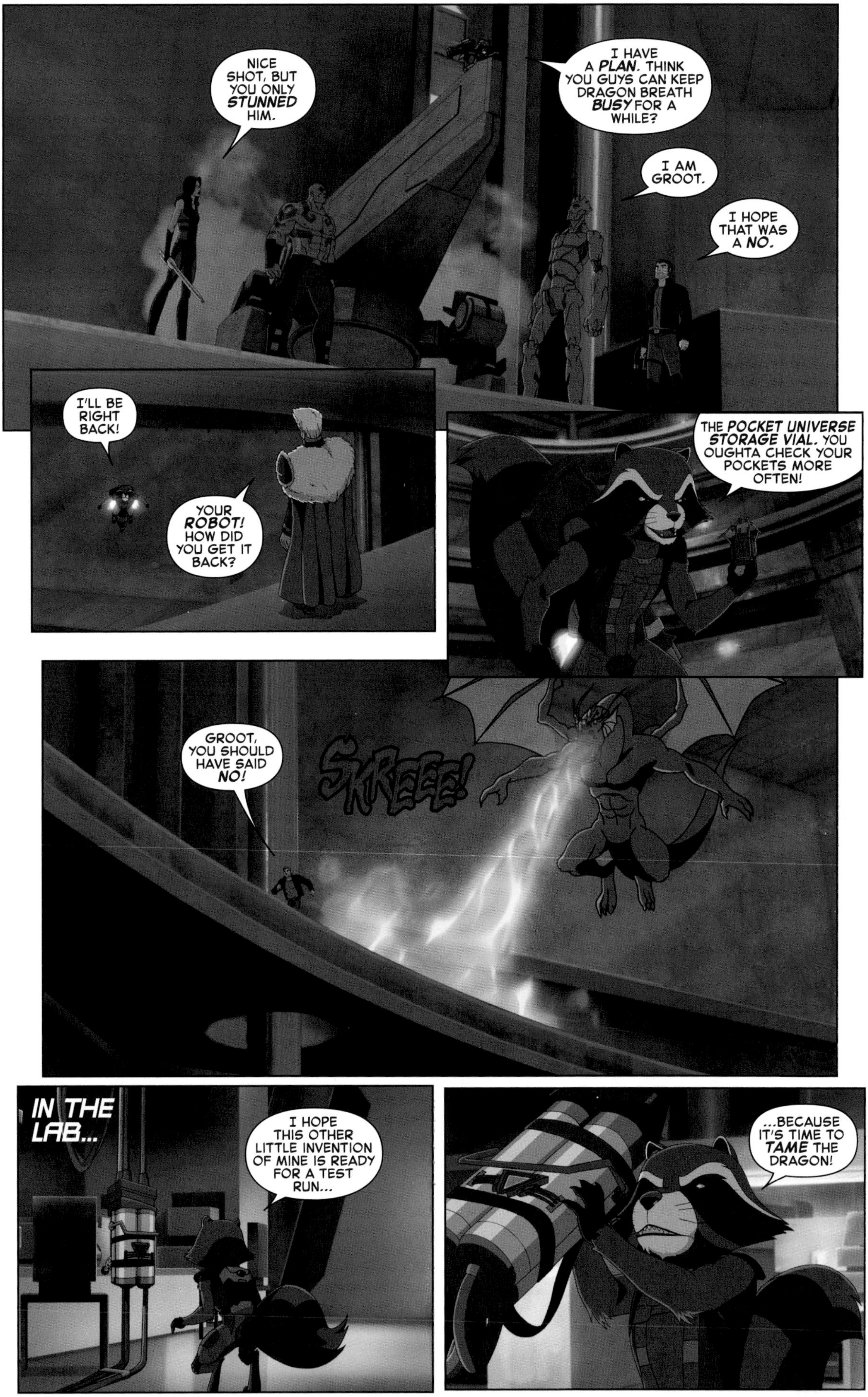
NICE SHOT, BUT YOU ONLY STUNNED HIM.
I HAVE A PLAN. THINK YOU GUYS CAN KEEP DRAGON BREATH BUSY FOR A WHILE?
I AM GROOT.
I HOPE THAT WAS A NO.
I'LL BE RIGHT BACK!
YOUR ROBOT! HOW DID YOU GET IT BACK?
THE POCKET UNIVERSE STORAGE VIAL. YOU OUGHTA CHECK YOUR POCKETS MORE OFTEN!
GROOT, YOU SHOULD HAVE SAID NO!
SKREEE!
IN THE LAB...
I HOPE THIS OTHER LITTLE INVENTION OF MINE IS READY FOR A TEST RUN...
...BECAUSE IT'S TIME TO TAME THE DRAGON!

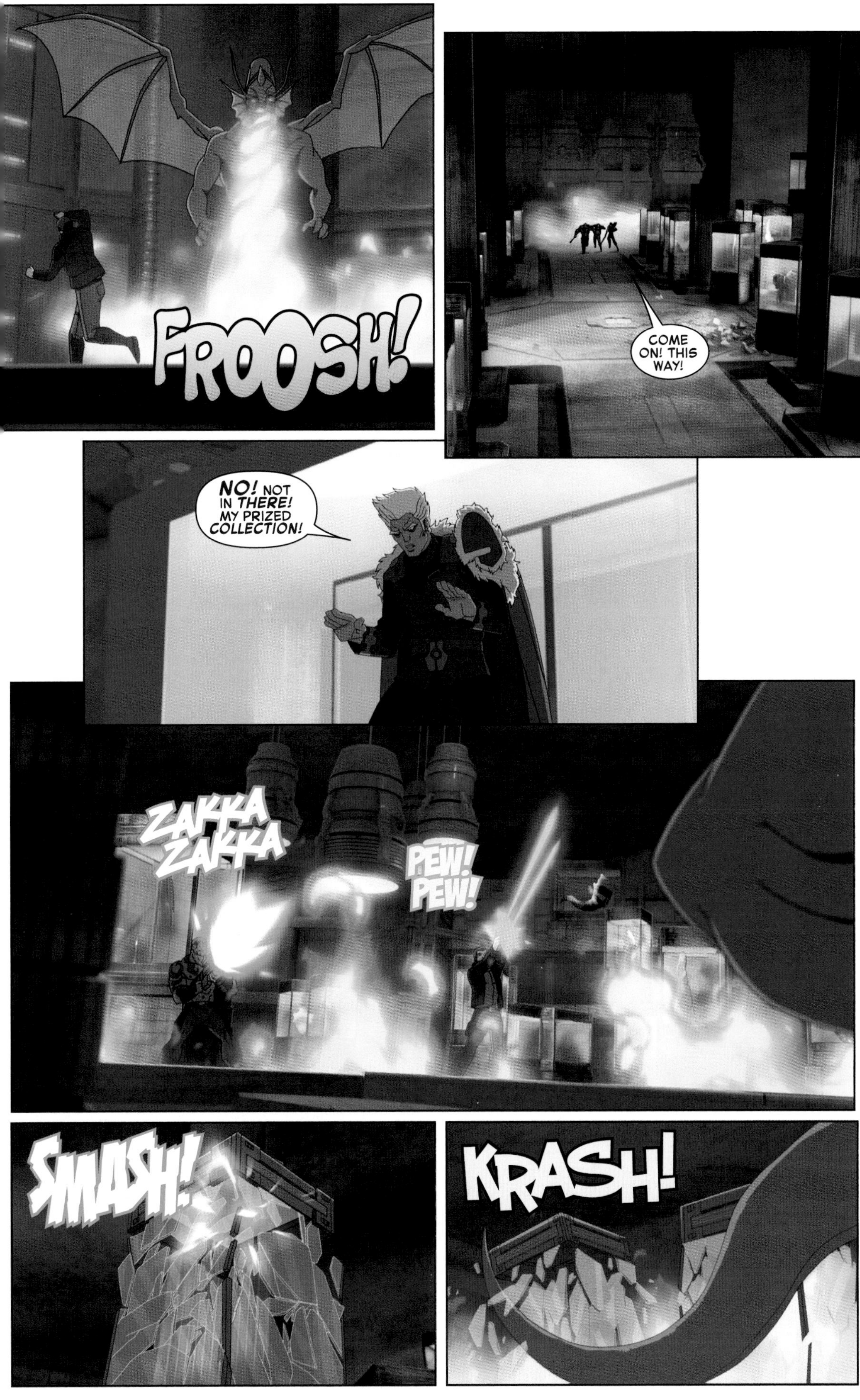
FROOSH!
COME ON! THIS WAY!
NO! NOT IN THERE! MY PRIZED COLLECTION!
ZAKKA ZAKKA
PEW! PEW!
SMASH!
KRASH!

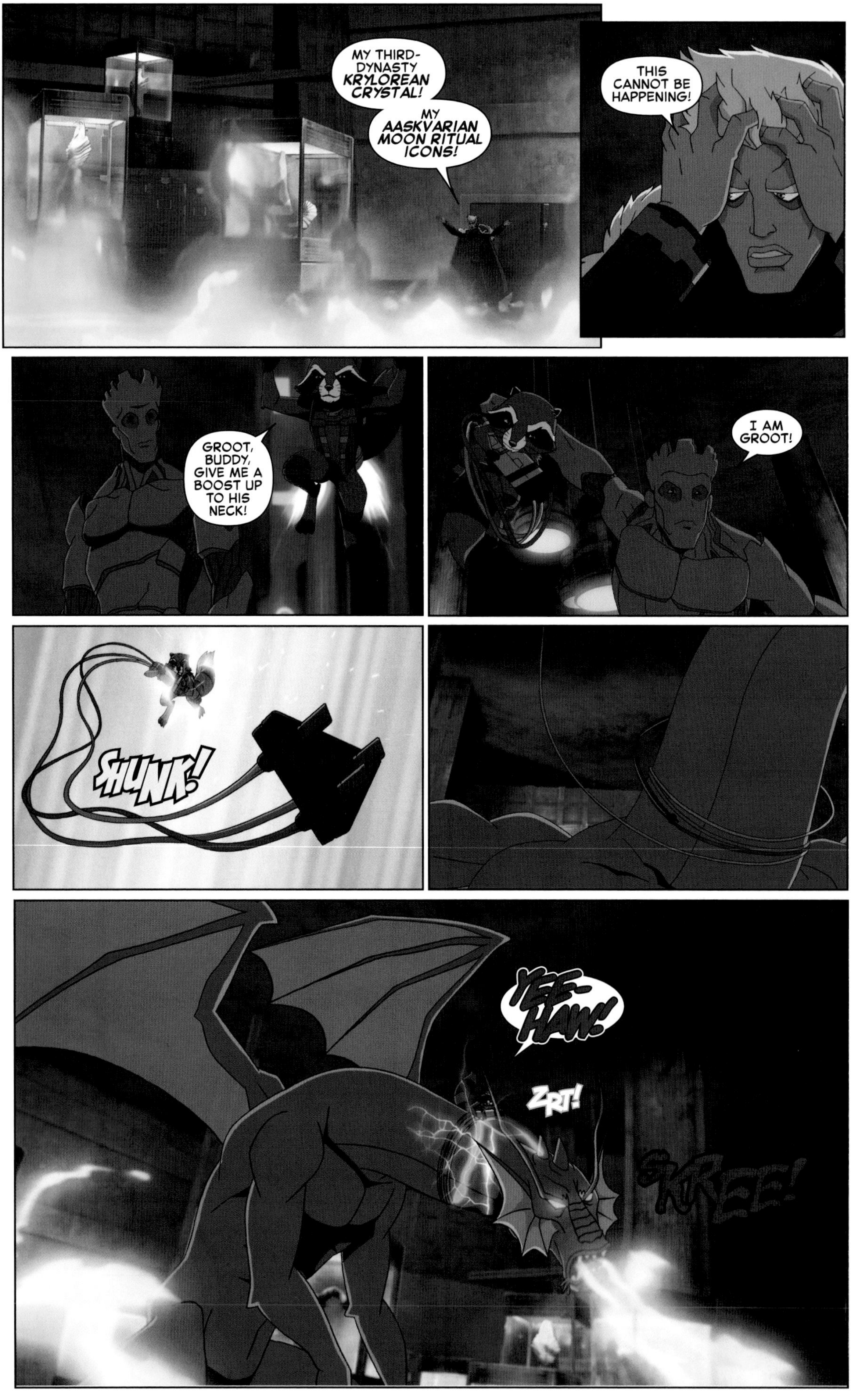
MY THIRD-DYNASTY KRYLOREAN CRYSTAL!
MY AASKVARIAN MOON RITUAL ICONS!
THIS CANNOT BE HAPPENING!
GROOT, BUDDY, GIVE ME A BOOST UP TO HIS NECK!
I AM GROOT!
SHUNK!
YEE-HAW!
ZRT!
SKREE!

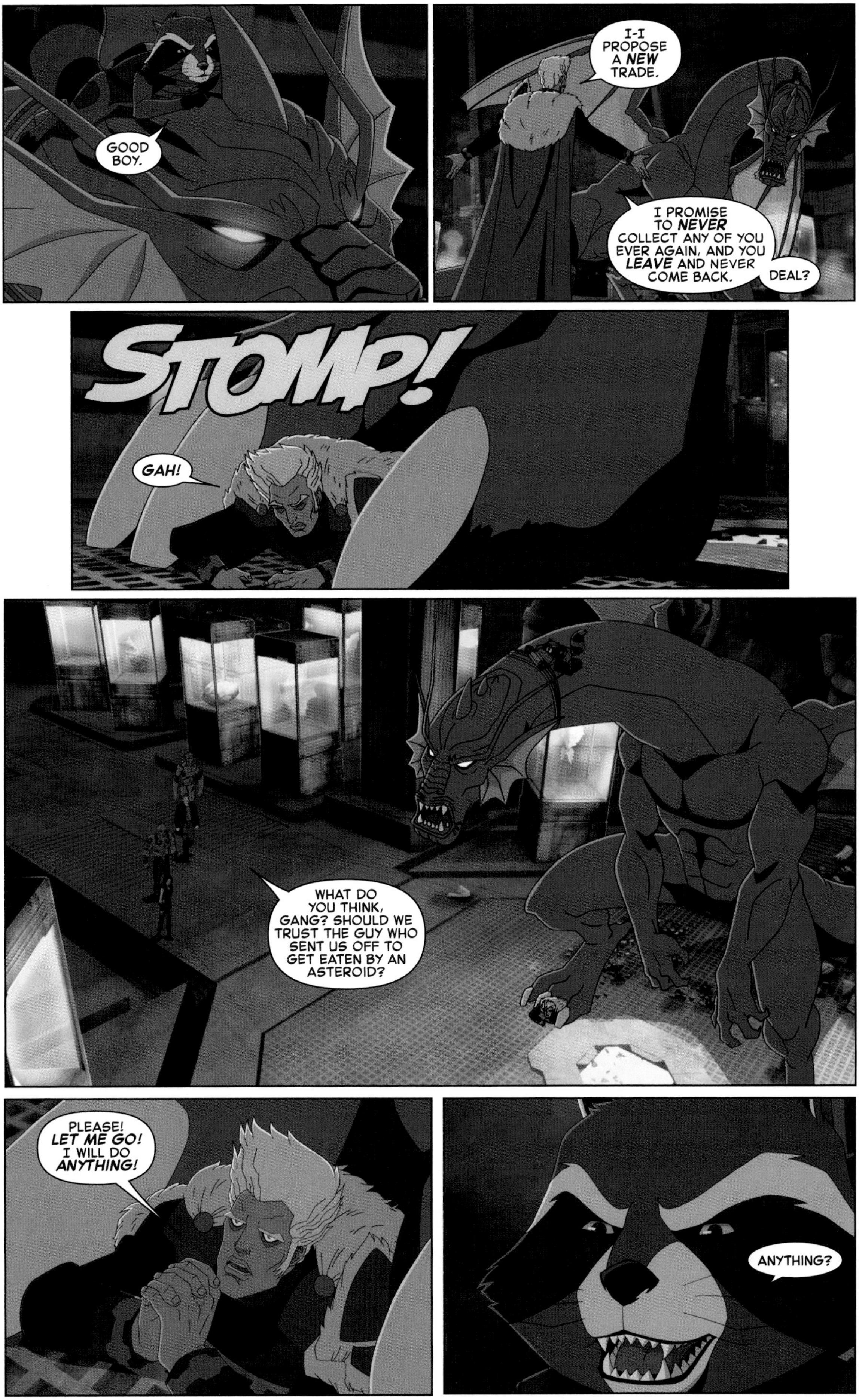
GOOD BOY.
I-I PROPOSE A NEW TRADE.
I PROMISE TO NEVER COLLECT ANY OF YOU EVER AGAIN, AND YOU LEAVE AND NEVER COME BACK.
DEAL?
STOMP!
GAH!
WHAT DO YOU THINK, GANG? SHOULD WE TRUST THE GUY WHO SENT US OFF TO GET EATEN BY AN ASTEROID?
PLEASE! LET ME GO! I WILL DO ANYTHING!
ANYTHING?

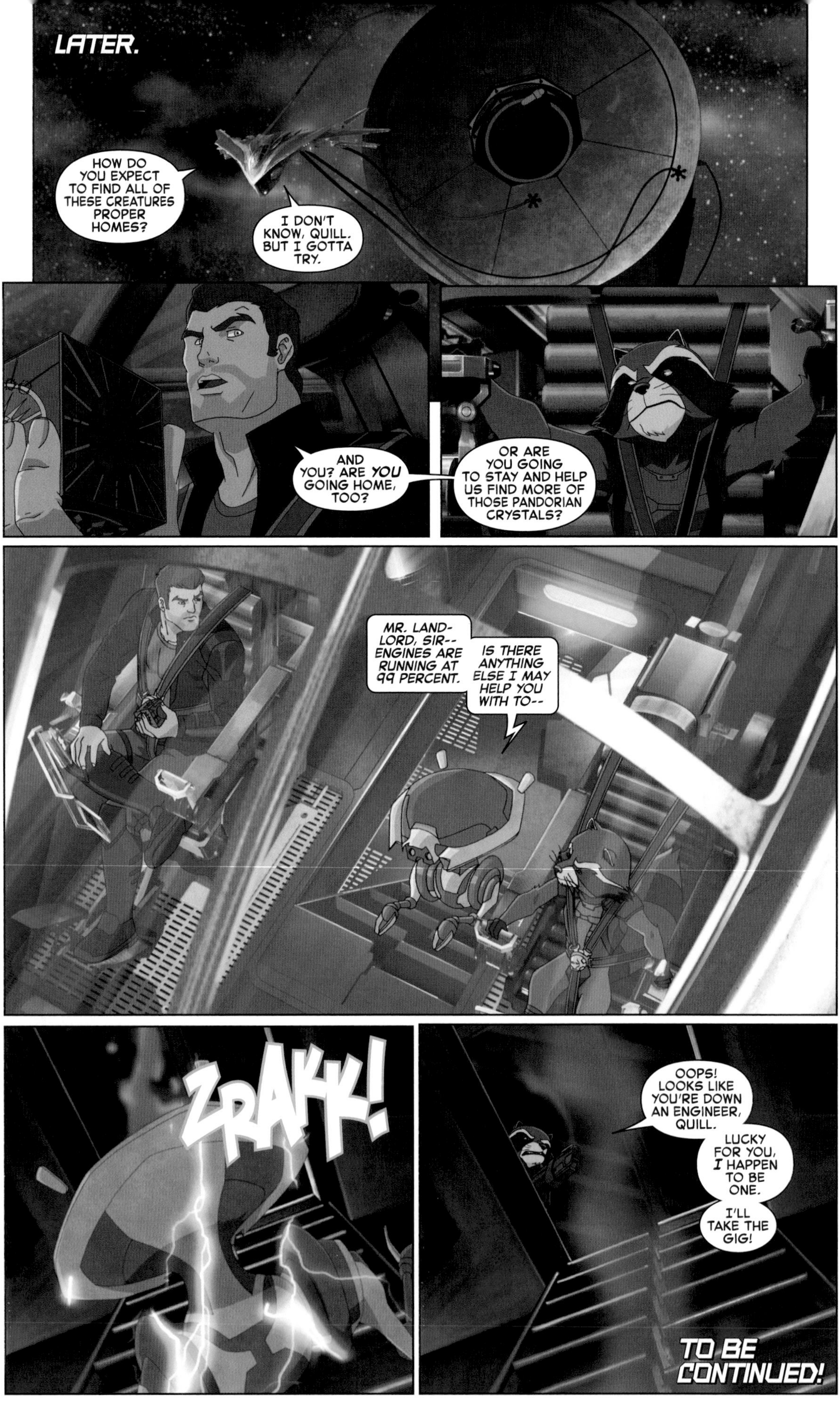
LATER.
HOW DO YOU EXPECT TO FIND ALL OF THESE CREATURES PROPER HOMES?
I DON'T KNOW, QUILL. BUT I GOTTA TRY.
AND YOU? ARE *YOU* GOING HOME, TOO?
OR ARE YOU GOING TO STAY AND HELP US FIND MORE OF THOSE PANDORIAN CRYSTALS?
MR. LAND-LORD, SIR-- ENGINES ARE RUNNING AT 99 PERCENT.
IS THERE ANYTHING ELSE I MAY HELP YOU WITH TO--
ZRAKK!
OOPS! LOOKS LIKE YOU'RE DOWN AN ENGINEER, QUILL.
LUCKY FOR YOU, *I* HAPPEN TO BE ONE.
I'LL TAKE THE GIG!
TO BE CONTINUED!

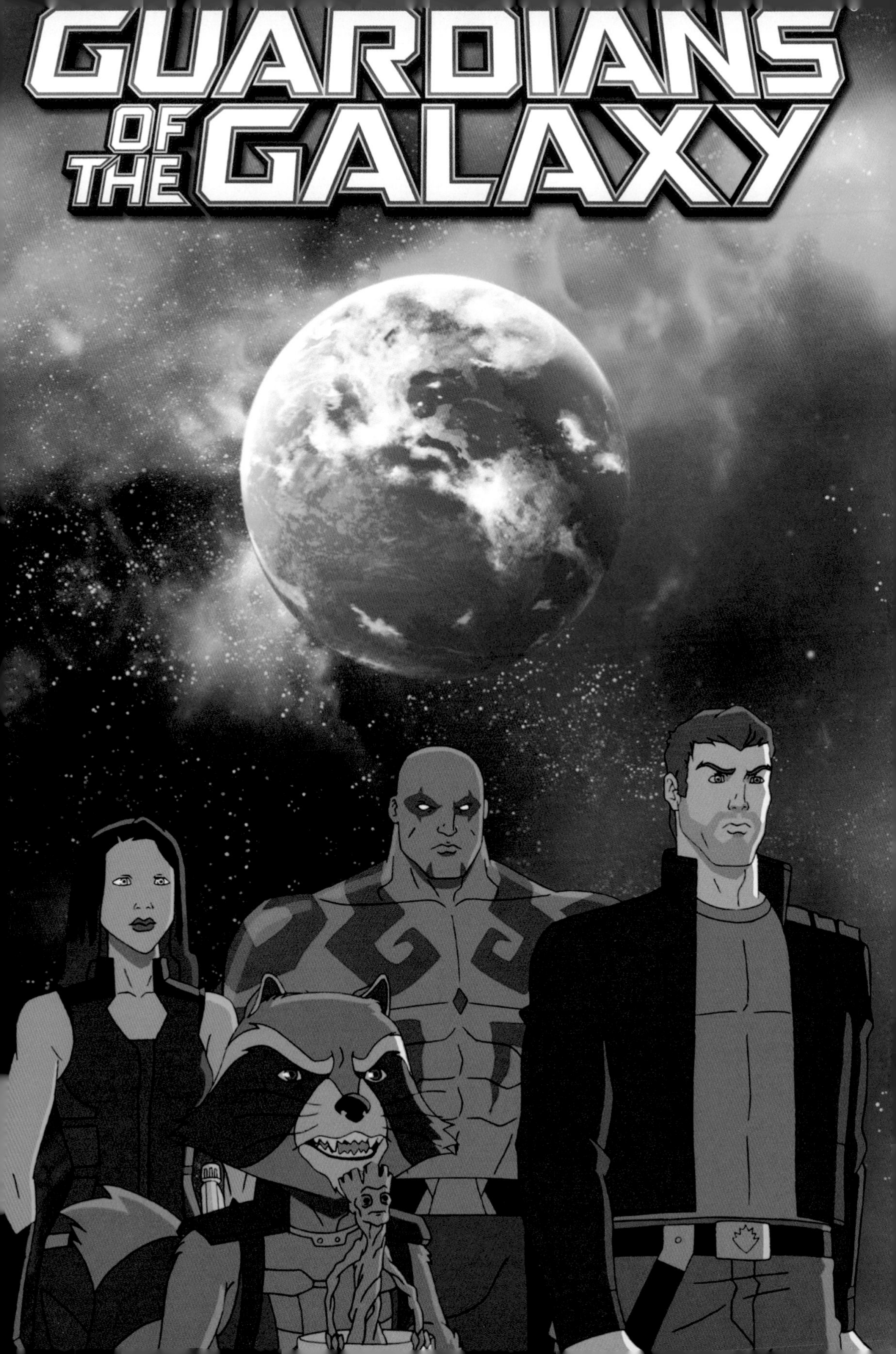
GUARDIANS
OF THE GALAXY

GUARDIANS OF THE GALAXY

COLLECT THEM ALL!

Set of 6 Hardcover Books ISBN: 978-1-5321-4069-3

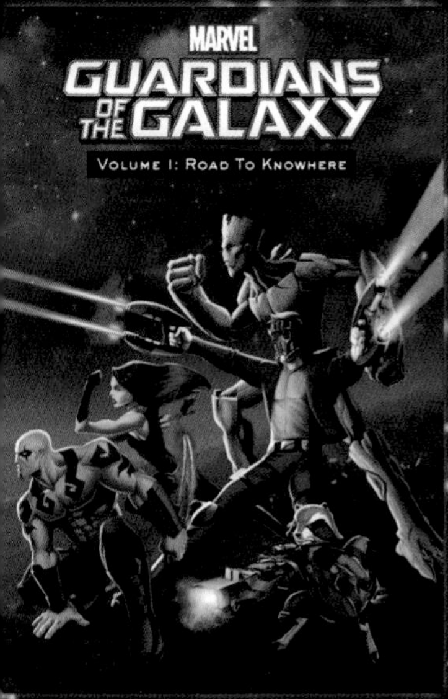
MARVEL
GUARDIANS OF THE GALAXY
Volume 1: Road To Knowhere

Hardcover Book ISBN
978-1-5321-4070-9

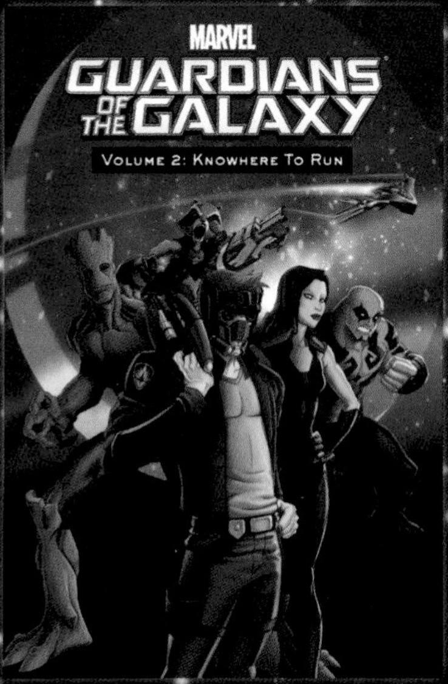
MARVEL
GUARDIANS OF THE GALAXY
Volume 2: Knowhere To Run

Hardcover Book ISBN
978-1-5321-4071-6

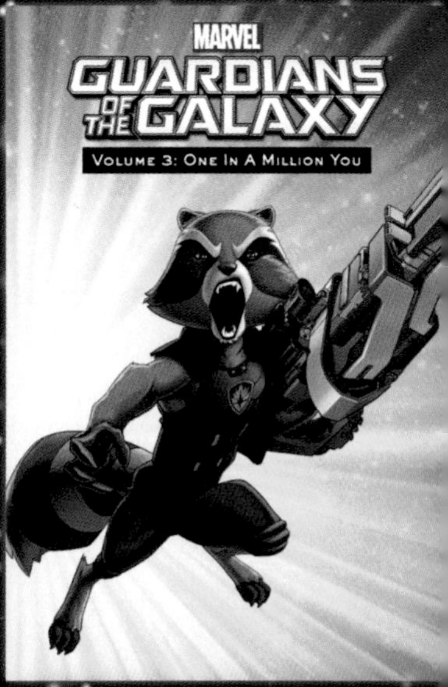
MARVEL
GUARDIANS OF THE GALAXY
Volume 3: One In A Million You

Hardcover Book ISBN
978-1-5321-4072-3

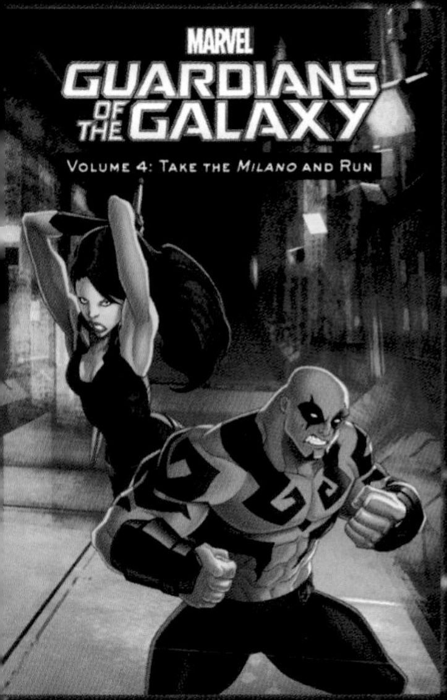
MARVEL
GUARDIANS OF THE GALAXY
Volume 4: Take the *Milano* and Run

Hardcover Book ISBN

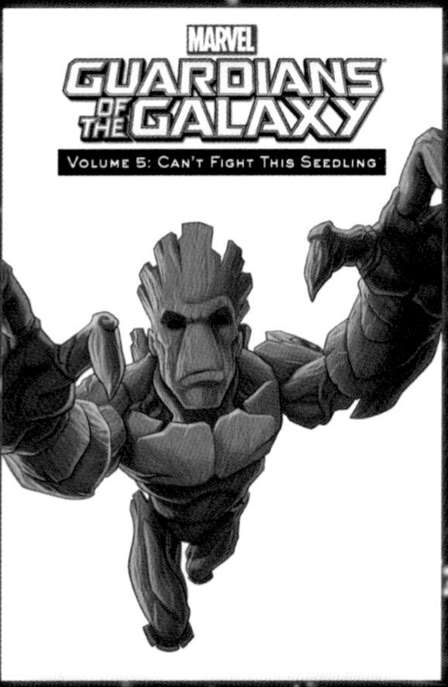
MARVEL
GUARDIANS OF THE GALAXY
Volume 5: Can't Fight This Seedling

Hardcover Book ISBN

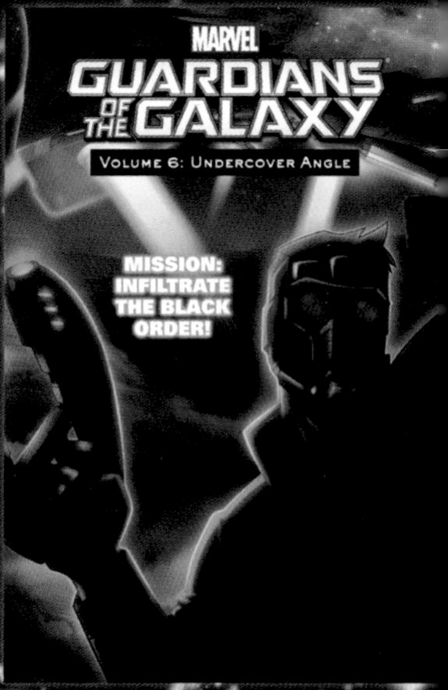
MARVEL
GUARDIANS OF THE GALAXY
Volume 6: Undercover Angle
MISSION: INFILTRATE THE BLACK ORDER!

Hardcover Book ISBN